OPENING MOVES

OPENING MOVES

Michael Thaler

THE MAKING OF A YOUNG CHESS CHAMPION

by

Barry Berg

With an Afterword by **Fred Thaler**

With Photographs by **David Hautzig**

LITTLE, BROWN AND COMPANY
Boston   New York   London

First Edition

With thanks to Jovan Miletic for checking the notations.

LIBRARY OF CONGRESS CATALOGING-IN-PUBLICATION DATA

Berg, Barry.
    Opening moves : Michael Thaler: the making of a young chess champion / by Barry Berg ; with an
afterword by Fred Thaler ; with photographs by David Hautzig. — 1st ed.
        p.   cm.
    Summary: Describes how chess champion Michael Thaler discovered and developed his talent
at an early age and learned to deal with both winning and losing.
    ISBN 0-316-91339-1
    1. Thaler, Michael, 1992–   Juvenile literature.   2. Chess players—United Stated Biography
Juvenile literature. [1. Thaler, Michael, 1992–   . 2. Chess players. 3. Chess.] I. Hautzig,
David, ill. II. Title.
GV1439.T43B47 2000
793.1'092—dc21
[B]   99-20803

10 9 8 7 6 5 4 3 2

WOR

Printed in the United States of America

Prologue

It was an unseasonably warm Sunday for March. The sun was bright; the temperature had climbed into the seventies and would touch eighty before the day was through. Residents of New York City's Greenwich Village were making the most of it, many spending a lazy afternoon in Washington Square Park. Families were picnicking on the grass, and bike riders and in-line skaters were enjoying the first really beautiful day of spring.

But not everybody in the park was relaxing. In one corner, an area reserved for chess, several serious games were in progress. This was not unusual; players and spectators gathered here whenever the weather permitted. The regular players were well known. They came every weekend, taking on all comers. They were good; they played fast and knew all the openings as well as the tricks and traps of chess. They almost always won.

On most days, each game had a few spectators, "kibitzers," who would watch the game and at the end

have something to say about which moves were brilliant and which were blunders. But today was different. Today everyone began to crowd around one table. They were watching one of their regulars play the white pieces against an opponent they did not know. The game was going more slowly than usual. Their friend, who always played with a smile, was frowning. He normally exuded confidence, but today his hand paused above a pawn, hesitated, and then hovered above another pawn as the frown turned into a scowl. As the morning grew hotter, their friend started to sweat. He traded pawns, then had to move his queen away from a trap. The kibitzers were used to hearing him give running commentaries on his games, pointing out what his opponent was trying to do and how he was cleverly avoiding the traps set out for him. Today he was quiet, and when he did speak, he muttered to himself.

His opponent, playing the black pieces, didn't talk at all. With eyes focused on the board, sitting on legs crossed under him to give some height and allow him to peer down at the pieces, he took his time evaluating each position. Then, when he made a decision, his hand moved with confidence and precision.

Bishops flashed, rooks swooped to attack and then backed up, and all the while, one black pawn moved inexorably toward the eighth rank. The crowd murmured with unease. Their friend was in a tight spot. Three more moves and he was down a piece. The black pawn had advanced and was about to be promoted into a queen. Finally, the man playing the white pieces relaxed his painful expression, shook his head in amazement, and smiled. He brought one long finger slowly to the top of his king and toppled it over, then extended his hand to the victor.

The crowd broke into excited comments as the newcomer had to rise up on his knees to reach out his hand, too. Someone in the crowd chuckled. The winner's tiny hand was completely lost in the massive paw of the loser.

"What's your name?" the park regular asked, astonishment still in his eyes.

"Michael," the boy replied. "Michael Thaler."

"How old are you, Michael?"

"I was six in February," Michael answered.

"You're in first grade, then?" The man couldn't believe he'd been beaten by a boy so young.

"No, I'm in kindergarten actually. Thanks for the game."

And with that, Michael Thaler smiled and skipped away. His dad, mom, and sister were sitting on a bench a short distance away, and really, he was supposed to be taking this Sunday off from chess. He'd been playing nearly every weekend, preparing to defend his title at the National Championship in Peoria, Illinois, in April, and today was supposed to be a family day in the park with no thought of chess. But when Michael had seen the players, he couldn't resist. He was glad his parents let him play at least one game. Michael enjoyed outings with his family, but he enjoyed playing chess more than anything.

The Best Puzzle of All

From the beginning, Michael loved puzzles. His dad remembers that when Michael was only two years old, they bought him a cutout puzzle of the United States. In no time flat, the boy could name every state just by looking at its shape.

He was a few months past his fourth birthday, still in preschool, when he discovered chess. Michael's mom, Linda, thought that since her son was so good at puzzles, he might enjoy chess, so she found a chess teacher named Barry Noble to introduce him to the game. The lesson was supposed to last forty minutes. Two and a half hours later, the teacher stood up and announced to a startled Linda, "I have never seen anyone learn chess so quickly!" Just as Michael had learned the shapes of all the states and how they fit together, he seemed to intuitively understand how the chess pieces worked together to control important squares on the board that could lead to checkmate. The teacher finished dramatically: "Your boy will be a master by the time he's ten years old!"

When Michael's dad, Fred, heard about the lesson, he asked his son, "Michael, did you enjoy learning how to play chess?"

"Daddy, I loved it! This is the best puzzle of all. Can I play chess again?" Michael could barely contain the excitement in his four-year-old body.

Fred and Linda looked at each other and shrugged. They had never seen their son this eager. Luckily, Michael's school, Corlears, had a chess club for students up to fourth grade. So that Monday, Fred walked into the chess club at Corlears and approached Jovan Miletic, a master player from Europe who coached the club. Fred asked if his son could join.

Jovan didn't think that was a good idea. "Of course it's wonderful that Michael learned the game and loves chess so much," the chess master replied. "But he's so young. Most of the other children who play are six and seven and eight. Why don't we wait a year?"

But Fred Thaler was persistent. "Let's just give Michael a chance. He wants to play so much."

Jovan finally gave in. The next weekend, Michael played his first game at the Corlears chess club and decisively beat a boy who had been playing for a whole year. Jovan was impressed. "I guess he can join our club," he said.

A month later, Jovan telephoned the Thalers. "I've been waiting for a boy like Michael to come along all my life," he told them breathlessly. "Your son is more than just good. He has an understanding for the game that I have never seen in a child so young. I think he might be a prodigy."

It was at this moment that Fred and Linda realized that chess was more than just a fun hobby for their son. They talked it over between themselves and agreed: If Michael was that talented at chess, they would do everything they could to promote his talent. That night, as Fred was putting Michael to sleep, he talked to him seriously about the situation.

"Michael, Jovan thinks you have the potential to be very, very good at chess."

"I know," Michael replied simply.

"Do you want to spend more time at it? Take lessons and study chess? And on weekends play in tournaments?"

"Yes, yes, yes, Daddy!" Michael exclaimed standing up in bed and jumping up and down.

So Michael's schedule changed. He still went to school every day, and he still took his weekly piano lesson. He still practiced playing baseball, so that when he was old enough he could play in Little League. But now he also went to chess club after school twice a week, and on Saturdays he took a private lesson from Jovan. And Fred played with his son regularly, teaching the boy everything he knew. Soon Michael began playing in school tournaments on weekends. His first big tournament, the New York Metropolitan Championship, came in January 1997, the month before he turned five. He won three games, tied two, and lost one. Even though he was still in preschool, his score was good enough to place him third in the kindergarten division, and he won a small trophy, which he proudly stood on his bedroom shelf.

That fall, Michael entered kindergarten at Hunter

Elementary School. Happily, Hunter had a strong chess program run by another wonderful teacher, Sunil Weeramantry. To his great delight, Michael was now surrounded by chess. In addition to a private lesson from Jovan each week, he took a lesson with the other members of the Hunter chess team from Sunil. Nearly every weekend brought a local or state tournament, and Michael improved so rapidly that he either won or finished high up in every one. His bedroom shelf was becoming crowded with trophies, and not all small ones, either. As the tournaments got more important, the trophies got bigger and bigger.

He also made a new friend, first-grader Arthur Wei. Together they competed in many scholastic tournaments. The crowning achievement came that year in Parsippany, New Jersey, where Arthur won the First Grade National Championship and Michael won the Kindergarten National Championship.

To Lose Is to Learn

That spring, with his second National Championship only four weeks away, Michael concentrated on his chess study in the evenings. He played games against the computer and also studied two games he had lost to one particular boy, Josh Tucker. Josh was one of the strongest players in their age group, and Michael promised himself that he wouldn't lose to Josh a third time if they opposed each other at the Nationals.

Michael, his dad, and Jovan decided that to keep sharp, Michael would play in one more tournament and then take some time off to relax. So the following Saturday, Michael entered an open tournament, in which adults played together with children, at the Manhattan Chess Club. He started off uncertainly and lost his first game to a more experienced player. At the break, Fred spoke to his son.

"You don't feel too bad about losing that game, do you, Michael?"

"Not really," Michael replied. "I didn't make any bad mistakes."

"And you know what I always say."

"Yeah." Michael smiled. "When you lose against a better player, you learn."

His second game was another loss. Michael had

developed an excellent position — in fact he should have won. But he took a lot of time thinking, and since each player in this tournament was allowed only one hour for all their moves, Michael lost because his time expired. Fred took his son outside for an ice cream. "Michael, you look tired. Let's withdraw from this tournament and just rest up for the last two weeks."

"No," Michael insisted. "I want to finish! You taught me not to quit, didn't you?" Fred couldn't argue with that, so he reluctantly let Michael play the last two games. Michael showed some toughness that day. He concentrated, played more quickly, and finished with a flourish, winning those last two games easily.

Lessons I Have Learned

Michael plays chess because he loves the game. But he'll quickly tell you that growing strong in chess has taught him to grow in other ways, too.

"I've learned seven lessons from chess," Michael declares. And while learning these lessons has made Michael into a champion player, they also apply to school, to playing the piano, and to baseball. In fact they apply to everything in his life.

LESSON #1: PREPARE

"If two players are almost the same strength, the one who has prepared better for the game will usually win," Michael says. He reads chess books all the time. He learns how the great players handle different openings, and he studies traps and problems that occur in the middle game. At night he plays against the computer—*Fritz 5* is his favorite program. *Fritz* always wins, but Michael is the one who keeps getting better. And Jovan continuously works on Michael's end game, so that Michael knows the most efficient way to checkmate his opponent or force a pawn to the eighth rank, where it will become a queen.

LESSON #2: RESPECT YOUR OPPONENT

Michael knows better than most other players that it is a mistake to underestimate your opponent. He knows this because when he first started playing, he wasn't even in kindergarten, and he was playing boys and girls in third and fourth grade. Some of those kids thought that a five-year-old wouldn't even know all the moves of chess, much less play a strong game. They were very much mistaken, and Michael has taken this lesson to heart. "Even if you are the stronger player, in any game your opponent can come up with a tricky combination and beat you."

LESSON #3: FOCUS

"When kids play chess, they move around a lot," Michael says. "They stand up and sit down, and talk to their opponents during the game. Also, when they've moved their piece, and their opponent is thinking for a long time, they get up and look at other games."

Before every game, Michael's dad reminds him how important it is to stay focused. "Your eyes should only be on the board. If your opponent tries to talk to you, what do you do?" Fred asks.

"Ignore him," Michael answers. "Just concentrate on the board."

In one game, Michael's opponent asked if Michael had won any trophies. Michael said yes, and they had a conversation about that. After the game, Fred spoke to his son. "That boy might not have done it intentionally, Michael, but he made you use up time on your clock during that conversation, and he broke your concentration!"

Michael learned a lesson that day. "I can be polite and have conversations before and after the game," he says. "During the game, I have to focus to analyze my position. Sometimes I sort of space out and waste time, and then I might lose. I have to always concentrate to come up with my best move."

LESSON #4: PATIENCE

"This is a hard one for kids," Michael announces. "You have to be so patient in chess. You have to develop all your pieces and build your position slowly, so you don't leave weaknesses for your opponent to attack." Michael admits that sometimes in the opening he attacks too quickly, with only a queen and maybe a bishop or a knight. "This can work when I'm playing against a kid who is just beginning to play chess, but it can get me in trouble with a better player."

Michael thinks for a long time before he moves. "What happened to me at the Manhattan Chess Club Tournament happens a lot," Michael admits ruefully. "Sometimes, even when I have a guaranteed winning position, I still spend a lot of time thinking, and I've lost a lot of games that way." Although losing a game for expired time might be upsetting at the moment, both Fred and Jovan agree that in the long run, Michael's careful play will benefit him. "Better to lose a few games now," Jovan advises, "if it means developing the habit

of thoughtfulness and patience at the chessboard." At another tournament, Sunil watched Michael, who had less than one minute on his clock, make eight precise moves to checkmate an opponent. "Don't worry about his slow play," Sunil advised Fred. "Your boy has ice water in his veins."

LESSON #5: DEVELOP A PLAN

"Jovan says this to me all the time. As I'm going through the opening moves, developing my pieces and making sure my king is safe, I should begin to analyze what my opponent is doing. Where are the weaknesses in his position? Is there a double pawn I can attack? Can I find a safe outpost for my knight or bishop deep in his territory? If I don't have a plan, I'll just make aimless moves, and then my opponent's plan may succeed!" Michael knows that "tempo" is extremely important in chess. You have to be economical with your moves. "Just like you shouldn't waste your allowance, you shouldn't waste moves. If, after the opening, you have a plan, then each move will have a purpose."

LESSON #6: WINNING AND LOSING

"Be a good loser, and don't brag when you win!" Although Michael has had a lot of success at chess, he's lost a lot of games, too. "When you lose a game, you have to forget about it," Michael advises. "Sometimes you'll blunder, or you'll meet an opponent who is just better than you. In a tournament, if you keep thinking about a loss, you won't be able to concentrate on the game you're playing and you'll lose that one, too!" And Michael knows it's to his advantage to make an opponent he's defeated feel okay. "Shake hands with your opponent if you win. Don't make him feel bad. That's just good manners, and besides, you don't want him to be discouraged because you want him to win his next games against other kids in the tournament."

LESSON #7: CHESS ISN'T EVERYTHING

As important as chess is in Michael's life, he knows it's just a game and there are other important things, too. Music is important to Michael. His dad is a composer and arranger, and there's a poster in his room of his grandfather, Mac Thaler, who had his own radio orchestra back in the 1930s. Sports are also important; Michael has his sights set on Little League baseball. And when he has a break in his schedule, just hanging out with his friends and not even talking about chess — that's important, too.

Defending My Title

It was the week of the National Tournament. At a family conference, the Thalers decided that Michael and Fred would go to Peoria by themselves. Michael's sister, Emily, had her own school schedule, and Linda was particularly busy with her work. But they would phone every day, twice a day if necessary, to hear how Michael was doing.

On Thursday morning, Michael woke up early. His suitcase was packed, and his traveling chess set was ready as well. At noon, he and his dad kissed Linda and Emily good-bye, and with cries of "good luck" ringing in their ears, they were off to the airport. They had to take two flights to get to Peoria, and Michael didn't like being in the airplane much. Taking off and landing made his ears feel funny. To distract himself, he mentally rehearsed some key features of his favorite Scandinavian defense. He would be competing against the best chess players of his age in the country. And since this was an elimination match, the winners of one round would face one another in the next round. So if Michael was good enough and lucky enough to win his first games, each succeeding match would be harder. And even though chess is a game of skill, Michael understood that luck does play a part.

As he sipped some juice to ease the pressure in his ears, he remembered a game in a tournament a few months earlier. He had decided to move his rook from the e4 square to e7. He moved the piece, punched his clock, then looked back at the board in horror. He had accidentally moved the rook to e6, where it could be taken by a pawn! It was too late to change the move. Tournament rules dictate that when you touch a piece, you must move it, and once you punch your clock, that move is final. This move couldn't have been more dumb. Michael lost the rook and took a minute to regroup. *Don't get upset* he said to himself, *and don't give up.*

After he controlled his anger at the mistake, Michael put up a terrific battle. The game went more than sixty moves, but his opponent's advantage of an extra piece could not be overcome and Michael lost in the end. A careless, unlucky blunder like that now could cost him the championship. And since his games also counted in the school team event, his careless play could cost Hunter the team championship, too. He would have to be more careful and alert than ever before. Also, as defending champion, he was expected to win. All the other kids would be playing their best against him.

When they got to Peoria, Michael and his dad took the day to relax. That night they went over some of Michael's recent games. If you want to be a champion, Michael knew, there are always more lessons to learn.

"Do you remember your game at the State Championships against Noah Belcher?" Fred asked.

Michael remembered the game well. He had played some strong moves but then lost because his time expired.

"Let's go over that one," Fred suggested. They set up the vinyl chessboard and plastic pieces, and Fred opened a looseleaf notebook in which he saved the notation of all Michael's tournament games.

"Noah was playing white; he opened with the queen's pawn," Michael began. "The first moves were pretty standard."

1) d4	d5
2) c4	e6
3) N-c3	N-f6
4) B-g5	B-e7
5) e3	0-0
6) N-f3	h6
7) B-f4	B-d6
8) B-g3	c5

"This is a very complicated position already," Michael told his father. "See the tension in the middle where the c and d pawns can each take each other?"

9) B-h4	B-e7

"He was pinning my knight," Michael observed, "and I had to break the pin. It's dangerous to let a piece be pinned for too long."

10) Q-c2	N-c6
11) B-d3	N-b4

"I think this was a mistake. He's letting me trade my knight for his white bishop, and I think the bishop is stronger in this position."

12) Q-d2   Nxd3 +
13) Qxd3   b6

"Now I'm developing my white bishop, and he can't oppose it."

14) N-e5   B-a6
15) b3

"That knight outpost is very strong for white," Michael admitted to his dad. "And here I made a bad move. I wasted a tempo with my bishop and gave up the pin."

15) . . .   dxc4
16) bxc4   B-b7

"This is part of the plan I formed when I traded the bishop for the knight. I have to open that nice long diagonal for my bishop."

17) f3   N-d5 !

"I thought this was a really neat move. White couldn't take my knight with his pawn, because then I could take his bishop, checking his king at the same time."

18) Bxe7   Nxe7

20

19) dc   bc
20) R-b1   B-a6
21) Q-e4   Q-a5

"Now I'm pinning his knight, which somewhat makes up for his strong outpost knight on e5. Also, he has to waste a tempo moving his rook again to protect the knight."

22) R-c1   R(f)-d8
23) 0-0   R(a)-b8

"He finally castles, breaking the pin, but now I've got both my rooks on open files."

24) R-f2   Q-a3
25) R(f)-c2 R-d2

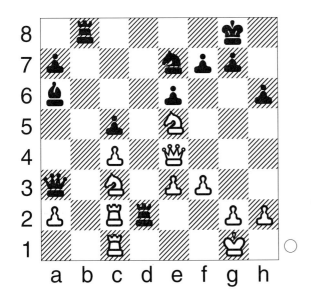

THE NOAH BELCHER GAME

"I was looking at this move for a long time. Too long, as it turns out," Michael added with an unhappy smile. "He can't take my rook because I'll take his other rook with my queen, with a check, and then capture his knight. Instead, he comes up with his only defensive move, which was a very good one, forking my rook and queen.

26) N-b1   Rxc2

"I have to sacrifice my queen, but I get his two rooks for it and a very strong attack."

27) Nxa3   Rxc1 +
28) K-f2

"And here I ran out of time!" Michael sighed woefully.

"It was still a great game," Fred countered. "How do you think it would have ended?"

Michael's eyes flashed excitedly as he described a plan that never came to be. "When Jovan and I analyzed it, we decided I can win with my twenty-eighth move, R-b2 +. He's forced to play 29) K-g3. Now I check with my knight at f5, he plays K-h3, and I attack his queen with B-b7."

His father nodded, agreeing with the powerful white attack.

"Only next time I have to play a little faster. Let's do one more."

"Michael, aren't you tired?" Fred asked. "You have a big day tomorrow."

"I know, but this one is a really interesting game against a much stronger player, Robert Shapiro."

"That was a great game, but it was another one you lost."

"Yeah, but to lose is . . ."

"To learn," Fred finished with a smile. "Okay, let's go through it quickly, then off to bed."

Michael set up the pieces. This was another queen pawn opening, which Michael defended playing black.

1) d4	d5
2) c4	c6
3) N-c3	N-f6
4) N-f3	B-g4
5) N-e5	N(b)-d7

"This was a really weak move," Michael told his dad. "I didn't realize it, but it loses a pawn a few moves later."

6) Nxg4	Nxg4
7) cd	cd

"Here's where I lost the pawn."

8) Nxd5	e6
9) N-c3	B-b4
10) e4	Q-c7

"I like that move a lot, Michael," Fred told his son. "You don't waste time retreating the knight. Instead, if white takes your knight with his queen, you can take his knight on c3 with your bishop, with a check. Then when he retakes with a pawn, you take the pawn with your queen, again with a check, and win the rook on a1."

"Dad, you're getting so good!" Michael said with a twinkle in his eye, and both father and son had to laugh.

   11) B-d2   Nxh2

"Here I regain my pawn, and attack his bishop at the same time," Michael noted.

   12) B-e2   h5

"I tempted him with this pawn, and he took it and got into trouble." Michael's eyes were glued to the board. "But I think I made a mistake taking that h2 pawn. I don't know what I would have done if now he just played g3, leaving my knight attacked by his rook with no protection. I can't move my knight to g4, because when he takes the knight with the bishop, and I retake with the pawn, he takes my rook with his rook, with a check, then picks up my second rook!"

"That's the difference between playing a tournament game and analyzing it the next day," Fred added. "There's no time to see all the combinations in the heat of play. Lucky for you, he took the pawn."

   13) Bxh5   g6
   14) B-e2   N-f3 +

"Here's the point of taking the h2 pawn in the first place," Michael pointed out.

15) gf	Rxh1 +
16) B-f1	Q-h2
17) Q-b3	Bxc3
18) Bxc3	Rxf1
19) Kxf1	Q-h1 +
20) K-e2	Qxa1

"Wow! Lots of fireworks here!" Fred enthused.

"And I had the advantage until this." Michael played the next two moves.

21) Qxb7

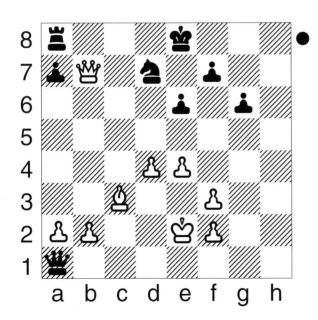

THE ROBERT
SHAPIRO GAME

21)...   N-b6

"This was a blunder! I was trying to save my a7 pawn. I should have let it go and played R-b8 and I would have been all right. Now my queen is out of the game, and my knight and rook are just defending each other and the a7 pawn."

22) d5   ed

"He's not giving me a chance to get my queen in the game."

23) Q-c6 +   K-f8
24) Q-d6 +   K-e8

"This was another mistake," Michael noted. "Jovan said if I had moved my king to g8, I'd have been able to draw the game.

25) B-f6   N-c8

"He has a checkmate here with Q-d8, which he didn't see. But he continued with Q-c6 + and then Q-a8, taking my rook with a winning game anyway."

"But it was a great game and he was a much stronger player than you," Fred replied. "You should feel good that you developed winning chances against such a strong player."

"I do, Dad." Michael flashed a tired smile.

Fred gave his son a hug. "Now to bed. We have a busy day tomorrow."

◆   ◆   ◆

On Friday, the National Championships began. Fred had to stay in an outer waiting room with the other parents — he couldn't watch Michael play, even from a distance — so with a final hug and kiss and the reminder, "Just do your best, son," he sent Michael into the playing room. There, hundreds of boys and girls from kindergarten through sixth grade were seated at long tables, facing one another in the biggest chess event of the year. Eighty-four of them were competing in the kindergarten division.

Michael took a breath, sat at his table, and shook hands with the girl opposite him. He could see by her first moves that she was a strong player, but she must have been nervous because she blundered badly on her fourteenth move, and Michael won the game soon after that.

"Whew!" said Fred when Michael emerged from the playing room and announced the win. "It's nice to have the first one behind us. Now, don't lose concentration, Michael."

The second game began — and Michael came out of the playing room after only fifteen minutes.

"What happened?" his father asked. The game couldn't possibly be over.

"It was weird, Dad. This boy — his name is Christopher Brzezianski — played f4 as his first move."

"That's not a usual move, Michael, but some people do play it."

"Yes, but look what happened to him."

Fred watched as Michael found a chessboard and quickly showed his father the game.

"I replied d5, then he played d4. I played c5. He took that pawn, dc. Since he was so exposed, I pushed my king pawn, e5. He took that pawn, too, fe. Now I brought out my king's bishop, taking his pawn at c5. And he moves his knight to h3!"

"Now, that's strange," Fred offered.

"Look what I could do now, Daddy." Michael stood up and hovered over the board with excitement. "I took the knight with my white bishop. He took back with his g pawn. Now I have a mate in four!"

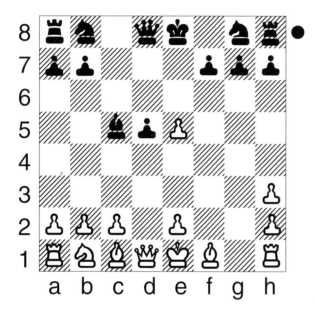

THE CHRISTOPHER BRZEZIANSKI GAME

"First, Q-h4 +."

"He has to move his king to d2," Fred observed, following his son's play on the board.

"Then I have Q-f4 +. He moves his king to c3. I check again with my queen on b4. He moves to d3. And now I play queen to d4 — checkmate!"

Fred was impressed. It was true that Michael's opponent had made some bad moves, but Fred had never seen his son win a tournament game so quickly. "That's great playing, Michael. But don't think the rest of the games are going to be so easy," he warned.

On Saturday, Michael had to play games three, four, and five. In game three, he played the black pieces against a very strong girl, but she didn't seem to know the variations of the Scandinavian defense. *Lesson number one: Always be prepared,* Michael said to himself as he developed a winning position out of the opening.

Michael's fourth game was a monster. Playing the white pieces he opened with his king's pawn, and his opponent responded with a variation of the Sicilian, a very complicated defense for white to

overcome. Michael spent a lot of time thinking, and this game lasted seventy-two moves.

Fred was a nervous wreck when Michael finally emerged from the playing room. "How did it go?" he asked. Michael flashed a tired little smile and put his thumb up. "I'm glad I didn't have to play this game in one hour," he told his dad, and Fred agreed. "That's a real problem for kids," he told his son. "You learn to play your school tournament games with a time limit of one hour, and then you play in a major tournament like this, and you have a three-hour time limit. It's really hard to adjust."

Luckily, game five turned out to be easier. Michael's opponent decided to push a lot of pawns, trying to trap one of Michael's bishops, while Michael calmly went about his job of developing his pieces. *Lesson number four:*

patience, Michael thought, as he noted that he had his queen and two bishops in the middle of the board while his opponent still had all of his pieces on the back rank. On the eleventh move, Michael announced checkmate.

Fred complimented his son at the end of the game. "Michael, you're playing very well. But don't lose focus. You still have two games tomorrow, and they'll probably be the most difficult ones of the tournament."

◆　◆　◆

Michael had some help on Sunday morning. After each round, the coaches of the Hunter team held a "skittles" session, in which they would analyze the games of that round. Today, Michael had the attention of his three excellent coaches, Anatoly Trubman, Mark Kurtzman, and Roman Krantz, to analyze his fourth game, which had been, so far, his most difficult of the tournament. They met early, before breakfast, and even though Michael had won, he learned where he had made some questionable moves and where he let opportunities slip by. "I think I've found lesson number eight, Dad," he told his father over a huge order of scrambled eggs and toast. "If you're going to be a champion, you can't do it all by yourself."

Michael's first game that morning was sharply contested. In the opening, Michael lost a pawn, but by midgame, he had developed a positional advantage, which he pressed until he won the game.

He seemed tired when he saw his father afterward. "Great going," Fred enthused. "Now I've got some good news and some bad news."

"What's the good news?" Michael asked blearily.

"You're the only player in this division who is undefeated. If you win the next game, you win the tournament."

"And what's the bad news?" Michael asked with apprehension.

"You're playing Josh Tucker."

Michael tried to relax during the break, but he was too excited and nervous to get much rest. He walked into the match, shook Josh's hand, and sat down in front of the black pieces. Josh opened e4, and Michael breathed a sigh of relief. He could play his favorite Scandinavian defense.

1) e4	d5
2) N-c3	d4
3) N(c)-e2	e5
4) N-f3	N-c6
5) N-g3	N-f6
6) B-b5	a6

"Can't let the pin remain," Michael murmured.

7) Bxc6 +	

Michael grimaced. He saw that he was about to lose a pawn. His sixth move had been a mistake.

7) …	bc
8) Nxe5	Q-d6

Have to get some positional advantage for it, he said to himself.

9) N-f3	B-e7
10) e5	Q-e6

Tricky, Michael thought. *He had my queen and knight forked, but now I've got his pawn pinned.*

11) O-O   N-d5
12) Nxd4   Qxe5
13) Nxc6

Michael groaned softly. He hadn't seen that combination, either. What was wrong with him? Now he was down two pawns and still had no positional advantage.

13) ...   Q-f6
14) Nxe7   Qxe7
15) R-e1   B-e6

Josh was playing very well. Michael knew that if he didn't turn this game around soon, he would lose.

16) N-f5

Attacking my queen. But Michael had good squares in which to place his queen, and the attacking knight was undefended.

16) ...   Q-f6

Taking the long diagonal and attacking the knight.

17) N-g3

Good, a wasted tempo. Michael quickly castled.

17) ...   O-O
18) d3

A conservative move. Michael had been preparing for d4, which would have been stronger for white. Michael brought his rook to the open d file.

18) ...   R(a)-d8
19) B-d2

A mistake? Michael's heart skipped a beat as he studied the position, then took the b pawn. Now he was only one pawn down.

19) ...   Qxb2
20) Q-e2

Another mistake? Michael couldn't believe his luck. He took the c pawn, and now he was even in material.

20) ...   Qxc2
21) R(e)-c1   Q-b2
22) Q-e1   R(f)-e8
23) B-c3

Michael saw that he had a choice here. If he took the bishop with his knight, he would end up trading queens and the position would be very even, almost certainly a draw. He wanted to preserve his winning chances.

23) ...   Q-a3
24) Q-e5

Careful. Josh was threatening checkmate. But Michael had a simple response.

24) ...   f6
25) Q-e1

Michael was pleased. White had lost another tempo, and the white queen was still under indirect attack. He could breathe easier. He had recaptured the two pawns and withstood white's recent offensive.

25) ...   c5
26) B-a5   R-d7
27) N-f5

Another mistake? Michael wasn't sure. He knew he couldn't take the knight with his bishop, because his rook on e8 was unprotected and white's queen would take it with a check. But white's d3 pawn was now unprotected!

27) ...   Qxd3
28) N-g3

Another wasted tempo for white! Michael was starting to feel more secure. He was now up a pawn, and his five pieces were in the center of the board on good attacking squares while his opponent's pieces were on the first rank and to the side. *I'd better not get overconfident,* he thought. *Lesson number two: Respect your opponent. Josh is a terrific player. If I let up for one second, he could checkmate me.*

28) ...   B-f7
29) Q-fl

White was again offering an exchange of queens. *Okay,* Michael thought. *This time I'm up a passed pawn.*

29) ...   Qxfl +
30) Rxfl   N-f4
31) R(f)-dl   Rxdl +
32) Rxdl   Bxa2
33) R-d6   R-c8

Michael was up two pawns now, and he could afford to give one back in order to get his rook behind his advanced passed pawn.

34) Rxa6   c4
35) N-e4   N-e2 +
36) K-fl   c3

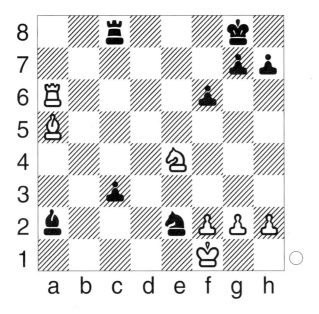

Michael's heart was racing. He could afford to sacrifice the knight because he had the fork with B-c4 coming up, where he would win the exchange for the pawn. After a lot of thinking, Josh took the knight with his king.

37) Kxe2   c2

Michael wasn't giving up the fork, but he didn't want to lose the pawn just yet. White's next move was forced.

38) B-d2	B-c4 +
39) K-e1	Bxa6
40) N-d6	c1=Q +
41) Bxc1	Rxc1 +

Michael took a moment to see what he had accomplished. He was up a rook. White had no attacking chances. He just had to play methodically and stay out of time trouble.

On move sixty-four, Michael placed his rook on the a4 square and announced checkmate. Josh put out his hand, and Michael exhaled a huge sigh of relief. He had successfully defended his title. In fact, he was the only player in all the divisions of this National Championship to play seven games without a loss or a draw.

His dad was beaming from ear to ear when Michael burst out of the playing room and announced the result. All their hard work had paid off. They quickly called home, and Linda

and Emily were very excited, too. They told Michael they were going to throw him a big party; they could not have been more proud.

At the awards dinner that night, Michael went up to the podium twice: once with the Hunter team, which he helped to win the team championship, and then to receive his trophy for winning the kindergarten division. Only one problem was left for Michael that evening. The trophy was bigger than he was, and it weighed a ton. How was he going to pick it up so his dad could take a picture?

Epilogue

There was no room on Michael's shelf for this latest trophy. With his family's permission, he stood it on the living room floor next to the front door.

All of Michael's family and friends congratulated him. He had a party and enjoyed his victory for the next few weeks, but then Michael came back to earth. He knows that tournament chess is going to be much more difficult from now on. "Next year I'll be playing in an older section," he says, acknowledging the challenge. "I'll be playing eight- and nine-year-olds, and some of them are very good." Still, Michael hopes that with hard work, he can be a chess master by the time he's ten.

"But I have other goals, too," Michael insists. "I want to play a piano recital at Carnegie Hall"— he's already played his first recital at Steinway Hall, performing a Bach minuet and a Clementi sonatina—"and of course I want to play Little League baseball."

But mostly, Michael just wants to keep having fun. "You know, I'm only six years old," he'll remind any adult who seems to have forgotten that fact. To translate his young life into chess terms, so far Michael has just moved a couple of pawns and maybe brought out a bishop and a knight. But the opening is solid. And Michael has a plan.

Afterword

LIFE AS CHESS DAD OR MOM

It was a cold, rainy, typically wintry New York day in January 1997 when Michael and I embarked on his first chess tournament. Although he was not quite five years old, his teacher of three months had said that he was ready to play tournament chess, so we woke up early that Saturday in anticipation of a nice quiet day of chess. We headed downtown to Manhattan Community College to play in the K-1 section of the New York Metropolitan Championship.

What we encountered took us both completely by surprise. The number of people—both students and parents—was astounding. Hundreds of students of all elementary-school ages were there to play this tournament. It was as if we entered a new world where chess was the magnet that drew all these children (and their parents) together.

There was noise and semi-chaos in the corridors. Latecomers were registering; tournament directors were frantically attempting to get the first round pairing completed so that the tournament could begin on time. Children were playing practice chess in the corridors, teachers were giving last-minute instructions to their students, and parents attempted to carry on conversations with other parents amid all the tumult.

Then the pairings went up for the first round. All the practice games in the corridors stopped; all the banter between parents and kids ended in mid-sentence, and there was a dash to the wall where the pairings were listed. Trying to get a glimpse of the sheet on the wall was like trying to read the newspaper over someone's shoulder in a crowded subway during rush hour.

Yet everything got done in its own way. The children went into the huge gymnasium, found their correct boards, and parents were asked to leave. The tournament director commanded in a bellowing voice, "Start your clocks!" With the exception of the sound of the clocks being struck, all noise ceased and all eyes became focused on the chessboards.

There is an explosion of scholastic chess in New York City. Many schools are adding it to their lower grade curriculum. Educators are recognizing its function as a wonderful learning tool. The benefits are obvious. Children learn to calculate; they learn to concentrate; they learn to win and lose. Their sense of spatial reasoning and mathematics improves. For those who think that chess is taking off only at elite private schools, I invite you to see some of the inner-city children competing in the various scholastic tournaments. Chess is a game that breaks down all stereotypes.

Michael has learned many valuable lessons through his chess tournaments. The value of sportsmanship, congratulating your opponent at the end of a match, whether you win or lose, is an important part of the game. He understands that hard work does reap rewards, and that the only way to really improve is to play higher-rated opponents — to "play up." He has completely bought the notion that "losing equals learning," which is one of the most important lessons for all improving players. I am grateful that he has found a passion at such a young age and has experienced success and failure, both of which motivate him to do even better. I know that these experiences will serve him well later in life, both in and out of chess. For these are essential lessons of life that go far beyond the chessboard, lessons that develop character and provide a road map to personal growth and fulfillment.

For a parent, the anxiety of competitive tournaments, both scholastic and adult, can be exhausting. Since I am not a skilled player and cannot help with moves and ideas, my function has been more as a trainee/parent than as a coach/parent. My role is to make sure that my son is well fed, well rested, and punctual. Even such things as reminding him to go to the bathroom before the game can be important since bathroom breaks cut into one's clock time. Michael tends to play slowly, making clock management crucial, and anything that can be done to conserve time can be the difference between a win and a loss.

Building self-esteem and confidence is another area in which a parent can be very useful. When Michael plays against a much stronger or more experienced player, we simply call it a learning game, taking the pressure off. In games that he is expected to win, it is important to remind him to respect the other player since anything can happen once the game starts. Win or lose, the parent can serve as a buffer. Lifting one's child's spirit when disappointment comes, congratulating him on achievements, and in general just being there and being a part of his world give a parent enormous satisfaction. The plane trips, the hotels, time spent playing cards or baseball between games, the excitement of the win, the disappointment of the loss — all will make indelible memories.

The bond that forms between child and parent is something that will not be forgotten in later life.

After every tournament, especially one that requires traveling, I return home thoroughly exhausted. Yet I would not trade the experience for anything. If you become a chess mom or dad, you will understand why. I highly recommend it. Good luck!